zenda

The Astral Summer

Dedicated to:
Mary T. Browne & Julie Chetkin
Johnny & Gena
and all Sacred Heart girls

Thank You to:
Bernice Sambade
Pam Amodeo
Janine Drozd
Mary Ann Wheaton
Caspar, Lupe & Charlotte an Amodeo Petti
Alan, Sonny & Betty

zenda

The Astral Summer

created by
Ken Petti and John Amodeo

written with
Cassandra Westwood

Grosset & Dunlap • New York

Copyright © 2005 by Ken Petti & John Amodeo. ZENDA is a trademark of Ken Petti & John Amodeo. All rights reserved. Published by Grosset & Dunlap, a division of Penguin Young Readers Group, 345 Hudson Street, New York, New York 10014. GROSSET & DUNLAP is a trademark of Penguin Group (USA) Inc. Printed in the U.S.A.

Library of Congress Cataloging-in-Publication Data

Petti, Ken.
  The Astral Summer / created by Ken Petti and John Amodeo ; written with Cassandra Westwood.
      p. cm. — (Zenda ; 7)
  Summary: Having retrieved all the pieces of her gazing ball and learned that she has two powers—kani and aura sight, Zenda goes on a retreat led by her friend Persuaja to learn the value of her talents and the responsibilities that accompany them.
   ISBN 0-448-43745-7 (pbk.)
  [1. Fantasy.] I. Amodeo, John, 1949 May 19– II. Westwood, Cassandra. III. Title. II. Series.
  PZ7.P448125As 2005
  [Fic]—dc22

                               2004021374

ISBN 0-448-43745-7   10 9 8 7 6 5 4 3 2

Contents

I can't believe the Astral Summer is only a few days away. So much has happened since the last one!

Each year on Azureblue, there is no sunshine for a whole month. Day and night look exactly the same: a dark sky glittering with stars. Most people on Azureblue use the time for quiet meditation and reflection.

This year, I'm going away on a retreat with some of the girls from my school. We'll be meeting girls from other villages there. My friend Persuaja is leading the trip.

At the retreat, we'll all be learning how to use our new gifts. Everybody on Azureblue receives a special gift when they turn thirteen. I got one gift early: kani, the ability to communicate with plants. Then, on my thirteenth birthday, I learned that I also had the gift of aura sight. I can see colors around people that most people can't see—but I don't know what they mean yet.

Having two gifts isn't going to be easy. I'm not sure if I'll be able to keep up with the other girls, but I'll try my best.

I need to think more positively, I know. I may not be psychic like Persuaja, but something tells me this Astral Summer is going to be one to remember!

Cosmically yours,
Zenda

Lightsend

"Torin! Torin! Torin!"

Zenda chanted along with her friends. Torin, the recipient of their energy, was focused on a pebble that had been placed on the tabletop in front of him. He was biting his lower lip, and his face was a bright shade of red.

"Come on, Torin," called Ferris, a tall, red-haired boy. "Show us what you've got!"

Torin made a soft grunting noise. The tiny pebble jumped up for a second, then landed back on the tabletop. Torin let out a breath, his face beaming with triumph.

Zenda turned away from the table and looked up at the bright blue sky. It was a beautiful day on Azureblue. White, puffy clouds floated overhead, and colorful birds flew from tree to tree in the woods surrounding the village's circle-shaped Commons. Just about everyone in the woods was in the Commons today. It was the second day of Lightsend, a yearly festival that lasted for three days, marking the sun's last days before the Astral Summer.

So much had happened since last year's festival, Zenda thought. For one thing, Zenda and her friends had turned thirteen. And like every thirteen-year-old on the planet, they had each learned which special gift they possessed deep inside.

Torin had the gift of levitation and was able to move objects just by thinking about it. Right now, making pebbles jump was about all he could do. But Zenda knew his gift—like all of their gifts—would grow stronger in time.

Zenda glanced at Camille. Her friend was quietly talking to a butterfly perched on her finger. Camille had hoped to get the gift of *enti*, which would allow her to communicate with insects. Her wish had come true, and Camille had spent the days since her birthday happily chasing after anything on six legs.

Next to Camille sat Sophia and Willow. Sophia's curly brown hair was speckled with paint, just like the overalls she always wore.

An artist at heart, Sophia was thrilled to learn that she possessed the ability to make sound paintings. Whenever she painted, the final painting produced a series of musical sounds. So far the sounds were rather screechy and erratic, but Sophia didn't seem to mind at all.

Willow's light brown hair was topped with a ring of tiny white roses. Willow had developed *koah*, the gift of communicating with animals, before she turned thirteen. On her birthday, she had learned that *koah* was her true gift.

Of the three boys that surrounded Torin, Ferris, the loudest of the bunch, had found out that he possessed the ability to teach. Ferris had shrugged, a little embarrassed, when he had told his friends.

"I don't even like school," he grumbled. "How am I supposed to be a teacher?"

Next to Ferris stood Darius and Mykal. Both boys looked very different; Darius was tall with dark hair and skin, while Mykal was shorter with shaggy blond hair and green eyes. But both had something in common. They both had the gift of *kani*, the ability to communicate with plants.

Zenda had something in common with them, too. She also had *kani*. And like Willow, she had developed her gift before she turned thirteen. Her *kani* was more developed than the boys', although she still had trouble controlling it.

On her birthday, she learned that she still had her *kani*. But she also had another gift: aura sight. If she concentrated, Zenda was able to see an outline of glowing light around people. The colors changed from person to person, and Zenda wasn't exactly sure what they meant yet.

Back at the table, Ferris had shifted his attention to the dessert table in the center of the Commons.

"Hey, Torin," he said. "Can you levitate that plate of chocolate cupcakes over here?"

"I could have a few weeks ago," Torin grumbled. "Right after my *harana*, I was sending chairs flying across the room. Honest!"

Zenda knew he was right. The *harana* was the secret ceremony where each of them had learned about their gifts. When the gifts first arrived, they were very strong. Zenda had seen auras everywhere, without having to think about it. But they calmed down a few days later. Verbena, her mother, had told her it always happened this way.

"You'll need time to learn how to use your gift before you come into your full power," she had said. "It is your body's way of protecting you."

Ferris had solved the problem of the cupcakes by sneaking to the dessert table and bringing them back himself. They were all gathered around the plate when the sound of jingling bells distracted them.

"It's the Sun Dancers!" Sophia cried.

Ferris jumped up on top of the table to

get a better view, and Zenda and her friends followed his example. Zenda had been watching the Sun Dancers ever since she could remember, and each year seemed just as exciting as the last. The dancers were the highlight of the Lightsend festival.

As a child, Zenda had loved them because they had made her less anxious about the Astral Summer that lay ahead. No one on the planet seemed to know how or why the mystical Astral Summer happened. Azureblue was known as being the greenest, most fertile planet in the solar system. How could such a planet survive a month of darkness? But the plants on Azureblue instinctively planned for the Astral Summer, storing up sunlight in preparation for the period. Many plants went into hibernation, stopping production of fruit and flowers until the sunlight returned.

Most Azureans went into a sort of hibernation as well, using the month for meditation, relaxation, and reflection. But for many children, including Zenda, the Astral Summer was a little bit frightening—day after day of darkness that seemed as though it would never end. That's why Zenda had always loved the Sun Dancers so much.

All paths in the village led to the Commons Circle, and now a line of dancers made its way down each path. The dancers wore robes and dresses of yellow and gold. Bright yellow sunflowers and marigolds crowned each dancer's head, and strands of gold bells adorned their ankles.

The dancers entered the Commons, their arms raised toward the sky. The lines flowed together so that the dancers formed a seamless circle as they danced around and around.

"They form a circle to honor the sun," Vetiver, her father, had always explained. "The dance reminds us that the sun will always return after the Astral Summer is over. They dance so that we will not forget."

Zenda felt her body sway with the rhythm as the dancers circled around and around. The jingle of the bells grew faster and faster. Then the dancers let out a low sound, a collective "Ahhhhhhh!" that rose louder and louder with each moment.

When the dance was over, the crowd clapped and cheered. From her perch on the table, Zenda saw her mother walking toward her. "We should get home soon, Zenda," she said. "There is a lot to do before you leave tomorrow."

"I'll meet you at home in a few minutes," Zenda replied. Verbena smiled and nodded. Zenda hopped down from the table. Camille scrambled down next to her.

"I should get home, too," she said. "I didn't even pack yet."

"I don't even know what to bring," Zenda said. "I've never been on a retreat."

Zenda and the other girls were going to spend the Astral Summer a few villages away on a retreat. They were supposed to spend the time learning how to use their gifts before the next school season started.

Mykal walked up and gave them both a sad smile. "I can't believe you both will be gone all summer," he said.

Zenda hugged Mykal. "It's only twenty-eight days, right? I'm sure it will go fast."

But that night, writing in her journal under the light of a moonglow flower, Zenda wasn't so sure.

———⚬⚬⚬———

I am a little nervous about the retreat. I've been away from home before, but never for a whole month! And Astral Summer makes me uncomfortable to begin with. I miss walking in the sunlight, the green grass, the bright flowers. During Astral Summer, everything looks like its been painted the color ob night.

The best thing about the retreat is that Persvaja will be there. I can't believe that just a bew weeks ago Persvaja was so sick. Now she looks just like her old selb, with those dark eyes that see right through you.

I went to visit Persvaja the other day. I told her I was nervous about the retreat, and she said, "You will learn new things about yourselb on this journey, Zenda, and that is a valuable gibt."

I shouldn't be so nervous. We will spend most ob the time meditating and doing sela. It sounds pretty calm to me. I'm sure everything will be bine.

I guess I'll bind out tomorrow!

Cosmically yours,
Zenda

———⚬⚬⚬———

Zenda closed her journal and placed it on her bedside table. When she turned back to the bed, she caught her reflection in the mirror on the facing wall.

Her whole body was surrounded by a pale light. The light looked like it was actually made of two colors—lilac purple and a yellow gold the color of sunlight. It was an aura—*her* aura! But Zenda had never seen anything like it. She got up to get a closer look, but the aura faded and then disappeared.

"What was that?" Zenda wondered out loud. Usually when she saw an aura, she got some kind of feeling around it—happiness, sadness, nervousness. But this time, she just felt uneasy.

"I'm sure it's nothing," Zenda whispered. But deep down, she wasn't so sure.

Retreat

The next morning, Zenda's uneasiness about her strange aura dissipated, and a feeling of excitement took over. Going away with Persuaja, Camille, and the rest of her friends was going to be fun.

Zenda quickly packed. In addition to clothing and toiletries, she was sure to add some of her favorite things: her journal and the small wooden box that held her gazing ball. Before she packed the box, she opened the lid and looked inside.

Her gazing ball, a small crystal sphere, glittered in the morning sunlight. Zenda liked to look at it from time to time, to remind herself it was real. For a long time, she had thought she might never get her gazing ball.

Every girl and boy on Azureblue received a gazing ball when they turned twelve-and-a-half. But Zenda had been impatient to see hers and had sneaked in to see it the night before her gazing ball ceremony. She had accidentally dropped the ball, and it had shattered into thirteen pieces that had vanished before her eyes.

It had taken Zenda six months to recover all of the shattered crystal shards. It hadn't been easy. But it had all worked out in the end. Good things had come out of the experience, too—like meeting Persuaja. The mysterious psychic lived by herself in the Western Woods. She had appeared to Zenda one night to help her out of a dangerous situation, and she had remained Zenda's friend ever since.

Thinking of Persuaja brought Zenda out of her daydream. She had to hurry, or she'd miss the wagon. Did she have everything she needed?

Zenda's gaze went to the top of her bed, where a small doll made of colorful fabric scraps sat, smiling at her with a stitched-on grin. Zenda walked to the doll and picked her up. She looked at the doll, then at her bag.

"I'm going to leave you here, Luna,"

Zenda said softly.

Luna had belonged to Zenda's grand-
mother, Delphina, when she was a little girl.
Delphina had passed Luna on to Zenda.
Granny Delphie had died a few years ago, but
Zenda could still sense her presence sometimes—especially when she looked into Luna's
eyes.

But Zenda was thirteen now, and the
other girls on the retreat, well . . . they might
not understand why she still carried a doll
around with her. Zenda gently placed Luna
against the pillows.

"See you soon," she said, feeling suddenly
sad. Astral Summer was a whole month long.
That wasn't soon at all!

With her bag finally packed, Zenda
headed downstairs. Verbena and Vetiver were
sitting at the kitchen table.

They headed outside, where a small
wagon, painted red, was hitched to two gray
horses speckled with white. Niko, one of the

workers at Azureblue Karmaceuticals, sat at the front of the wagon, holding the horses' reins. Vetiver took Zenda's bag and placed it in the wagon. All three of them climbed in the back, and Niko got the wagon moving.

When they arrived at the Commons, Zenda saw two larger horse-drawn wagons. One wagon was loaded with bags and sacks. The other, Zenda could see, held Camille and Sophia. Several other girls Zenda recognized were preparing to board.

Camille waved to Zenda from the wagon. Zenda waved back as Niko brought the horses to a stop. Zenda jumped out and ran toward the wagon.

A tall woman with long, dark hair approached. She wore a deep purple dress with flowing sleeves. Amulets and chains hung around her slender neck. Her midnight blue eyes glowed warmly at Zenda.

"Persuaja!" Zenda cried. She hugged her friend, and the myriad of bracelets on

Persuaja's arms jingled.

"I am so glad you are here, Zenda," Persuaja said. "And I must thank you. I would not be leading the retreat this year if you had not helped the healers discover the cause of my illness."

Zenda blushed. It had felt so good, so right to help Persuaja that she felt awkward being thanked for it.

"I'm glad, too," Zenda said. "I don't think I could do this without you."

"Of course you can, Zenda," Persuaja said, smiling slightly this time. "I thought you would have learned something from your gazing ball by now."

At that moment, a slight girl with pale blond hair appeared. She ignored Zenda and looked up at Persuaja.

"I checked the list of supplies like you asked me to," she said softly. "Everything is ready."

"Thank you, Astrid," Persuaja said.

Astrid nodded and walked back to the wagon.

Zenda didn't know Astrid very well. The shy, quiet girl had spent most of the school year shadowing Alexandra White. Alexandra and Zenda had only just become friends after a long rivalry.

"You know Astrid?" Zenda asked.

"I thought you may have heard," Persuaja said. "Astrid discovered she had the gift of psychic powers at her *harana*. She is the only one in the village to develop such a power. I will be tutoring her in the months ahead."

A tiny twinge of jealousy tweaked Zenda. Persuaja was something of a recluse, and being her friend had always made Zenda feel special. Was Astrid going to take her place?

Then one of Zenda's musings came to mind: *Jealousy is the lock that closes your mind and heart; understanding is the key that opens them.*

There was no reason to be jealous of Astrid, of course. Persuaja would be a friend and mentor to both of them. She had plenty of strength and wisdom to go around. Zenda took a deep breath and smiled.

"Let me know if you need help, too," Zenda said.

"Right now I need you to get on that wagon," Persuaja said, smiling. "We must get moving!"

Zenda felt a tap on her shoulder and turned to see her parents behind her.

"We loaded your bag on the wagon," Vetiver said. He handed her a sack of muffins and cookies. "I took this out so you could eat on the way."

"Thanks," Zenda said, giving her father a hug.

Verbena grabbed her next, kissing both her cheeks. Zenda saw tears glittering in her mother's eyes.

"We'll miss you, Zenda," she said.

"I'll miss you, too," Zenda said, her own tears beginning to form. She tried to hold them back, not wanting to let the other girls see her cry.

"I need all girls on the wagon now, please," Persuaja announced.

Zenda took the sack of muffins and gave her parents each one more hug. Vetiver helped her up on the wagon, and she sat between Camille and Sophia.

The parents of all the girls gathered around the wagon. The wagon driver, a young woman with a long blond ponytail, got the horses going.

Girls and parents exchanged shouts of "Good-bye!" and "Miss you!" as the wagons left the Commons Circle. Like most of the girls, Zenda kept her eyes on her mother and father until they were no longer in sight. Then she turned to her friends.

"Hey, Zenda! Guess what?"

Zenda turned to see Alexandra White at the back of the wagon, seated next to Astrid and their friend Gena. Alexandra smiled warmly at Zenda.

"What?" Zenda called back.

"I just had my *harana* two days ago, and I have *kani*!" Alexandra replied. "Just like you! We're going to be in the same classes next year!"

A year ago, Zenda would have been distraught over the news, but today she smiled.

"You're going to be great at it," Zenda said.

"I hope so," Alexandra replied. "Did you hear about Astrid's psychic powers? Isn't that cool?"

Zenda nodded. "That's pretty amazing, Astrid."

"Thanks," Astrid said in a quiet voice. Then she looked away.

The girls spent most of the long trip chatting excitedly about their *harana* ceremonies, their gifts, and what might happen during the Astral Summer. Before Zenda knew it, Persuaja announced that they had arrived. Zenda craned her neck to see past the horses.

A circle of wooden huts sat on a green field. Most were small, and one was shaped like a long rectangle. The circle was bordered by the road on one side and a lush green forest on the other. Several other wagons had arrived, and girls in colorful clothing walked among the huts.

The wagon driver led them into the tiny village and stopped next to one of the cabins.

"You girls will be staying here," Persuaja announced. "Each village has its own cabin. Please set up your belongings and get used to the lay of the land while it is still light. Sunset is in one hour. We will all meet in the center circle then."

Zenda and the others quietly climbed out of the wagon. There was something about the place—like a blanket of calm and quiet— that immediately put a hush over them. They unloaded their bags and walked into their cabin, curious.

The long cabin was sparsely furnished: four simple cots along each wall, with a large wooden trunk at the foot of each cot. There were no rugs on the smooth wood floor. At the end of the cabin was a doorway leading to a bathroom.

"I claim this one!" Sophia cried, breaking the silence. She jumped on a cot underneath a window.

Zenda and Camille took the cots next to Sophia, and Willow rounded out the row. On the other side of the room, Alexandra and Astrid claimed their cots, along with Gena and Mai, a quiet girl with short, dark hair whom Zenda did not know very well.

The girls unpacked their clothes and belongings. After a while, Sophia looked outside.

"I think it's time," she said. "The other girls are out there."

The girls from Zenda's village instinctively

clumped together as they made their way to the center of the circle. The girls from the other villages seemed to be doing the same. Zenda scanned their faces; they looked very much like the girls from her own village. The same pale faces, brown faces, sun-kissed faces; long hair, short hair, curly hair, straight hair; eyes the color of spring grass and eyes the color of the sea. Every head was crowned with a ring of flowers, a tradition around the planet.

To Zenda's relief, they all looked just as apprehensive and curious as she felt. The girls sat cross-legged in the grass, facing Persuaja in the center of the circle.

Just the sight of Persuaja was enough to quiet the girls down. When everyone was settled, Persuaja addressed them.

"In a few moments, the sun will set, and the Astral Summer will began," she said. "You are here to use this time wisely. There will be some structure to your days here. Meals will be served in that cabin—" Persuaja pointed to the largest of the cabins. "And you are expected to attend each meal when the meal chimes ring.

"When the Astral Summer is over, each of you will begin to study and train to use your gift," Persuaja continued. "The purpose of this retreat is to ground and calm your spirit before training begins. Each of you will receive a schedule of meditation and *sela* instruction, which will be available each day. At other times, you are free to do what you wish. Dream, dance, write, sing—this is your time. Use it wisely."

Four women stepped into the circle. One was the young blonde who had been driving the wagon.

"Let me introduce the retreat leaders," Persuaja began. She pointed to the blonde and to another young woman who wore her light brown hair in two braids. "Sabra and Celine know the area very well. They will be available to take you on walks or hikes."

Next, Persuaja pointed to a small, slim

woman who reminded Zenda of her own mother, although this woman's brown hair was cut short. "Miyo is our *sela* instructor," Persuaja said. Then she turned to an older woman with a pleasant, round face and curly red hair. "And Kaveri leads the meditation sessions."

Zenda started to relax. The instructors all looked friendly and approachable, like her teacher from last year, Marion Rose.

"And now for the rules," Persuaja said. "I trust that you will treat one another with respect and courtesy.

"I also trust that you will use caution when exploring the grounds," Persuaja continued. "The nearby woods can be quite peaceful. But no one is to enter them without a partner. And more importantly, the woods are off limits after midnight. The rendulla flower grows here.

"The rendulla is an endangered plant," Persuaja went on. "It blooms after midnight.

The flower must not be disturbed when it is blooming. It has very unique and powerful properties."

Before Zenda could ponder this, Persuaja motioned for the girls to rise.

"Time for sunset," Persuaja said. "You may want to watch this. It will be the last time you will see the sun's rays for twenty-eight days."

The girls stood up and turned toward the horizon. They watched in silence as the sun slowly sank behind the trees, streaking the sky with deep purple and red strokes.

"It's so beautiful," Zenda whispered.

And then, quite suddenly, the color of the sky deepened to a rich, deep black. A few silver stars studded the darkness.

"Good-bye, sun," Zenda said quietly. She closed her eyes and tried to conjure up a picture of the sunset.

She did not want to forget.

As the Astral Summer settled above them, Sabra and Celine walked among the girls, handing each one a glowing white moon-flower. Then they led the girls to the large cabin, where they ate earthy mushroom crepes, brown rice, and salad, followed by rich chocolate brownies.

Exhausted from their long trip, all of the girls returned to their cabin. Astrid, Willow, and Mai fell asleep right away. Zenda sat on the floor by Camille's cot, talking to her friend in whispers.

"Everything feels so different," Zenda said. "But it's nice here, too. Peaceful."

Camille nodded. "I know. I think we'll have a good month. It will probably be over before we know it."

Camille yawned, and Zenda climbed back into her cot.

"Good night, Cam," she said softly.

"Good night, Zen," her friend replied.

Zenda woke up to find Camille

shaking her by the shoulders.

"Zenda, the breakfast chimes are ringing!" Camille said urgently. "We all slept too long."

Zenda sat up, rubbing her eyes. Everyone in the cabin was scrambling to get dressed. Only Mai seemed to be missing.

"Thorns!" Zenda exclaimed. She hurriedly changed into the first dress on top of her folded pile of clothes, a short-sleeved green dress with an ankle-length skirt. She ran a brush through her long, curly hair, only to get it stuck in a mess of tangles.

"Come on, Zen," Sophia said.

Sighing, Zenda put down the brush and grabbed the flower crown she had worn the day before, now a limp ring of daisies. Then she followed the others outside.

They all stopped for a moment and looked up. It took some getting used to, waking up to a star-studded night sky. Then, without a word, they picked up the pace and headed to the meal cabin.

"Hey, Astrid," Sophia teased. "Can you use your psychic powers to tell us what we're having for breakfast?"

"It doesn't work like that," Astrid said curtly.

"Come on, take a guess," Sophia said.

"I don't want to," Astrid said.

At that moment, a small tree branch crashed to the ground right next to them. Zenda jumped. Astrid looked more startled than any of them. She turned and walked quickly ahead of the group.

The girls entered the meal hall. Oil lamps hung from the walls, illuminating the room with dim light. Many of the other girls were already seated at tables, eating thin pancakes wrapped around syrupy fruit and drinking glasses of what looked like mango juice. Zenda's stomach began to rumble, and she and the others went to the food table and piled their plates high. Then they all sat down at an empty wooden table and began to eat. Astrid and Gena flanked Alexandra, as they always did back at school.

Mai walked up a few minutes later and put down a tray of food.

"Sorry," she said, sitting down. "I got up early to go meditate on the hill. I'm used to doing it at home. I hope I didn't wake anyone."

"Maybe you should have," Sophia said, yawning. "We all woke up late."

"That's one of the things I hate about Astral Summer," Gena complained. "I never know what time it is."

"I might have an idea," Camille said. She reached into the pocket of her skirt and took out a small insect with a thin yellow body and long legs.

"Ew!" Gena shrieked.

"Sorry," Camille said, slipping the bug back into her pocket. "I just wanted to show you."

"It's a harp cricket, isn't it?" Astrid

asked in her quiet voice.

Camille's face took on the excited glow that it always did when she talked about her favorite subject. "That's right. I did some research before we came out here," she said. "The harp cricket chirps every day at noon. And there's a beetle that makes a clicking noise at seven in the morning. That's the one I really need to find, but I haven't seen one yet."

"I get it," Zenda said, impressed. "Kind of like an insect alarm clock."

"Exactly!" Camille said, beaming. "I just hope it works."

"I think it's an amazing idea," Alexandra said. She stood up from her seat. "Does anybody want some more juice? I'm going to get some."

"I'll go with you," Astrid said, joining her friend.

When she came back to the table, Alexandra wore an excited look on her face.

"Hey, Zenda, guess what?" she said. "I

just met some girls from the other villages. A bunch of girls with *kani* are going to meet after lunch. I said they could meet in our cabin. Isn't that great?"

What was it like to be so outgoing? Zenda wondered. Alexandra met new people so easily. But Zenda was always too shy to introduce herself. While Zenda pondered this, Sabra walked into the room.

"We could use some help with the dishes after meals," she said. "Any volunteers?"

Zenda raised her hand. The idea of having a job to do appealed to her. It made her feel useful.

"I'm going to try to find that beetle, Zen," Camille said. "I hear they live under logs. And I want to find one before tomorrow morning."

"Right," Zenda said. "See you later?"

Camille smiled. "Of course."

Willow and Mai also volunteered for dish duty. The three of them followed Sabra into the kitchen along with a group of girls from the other cabins.

Sabra pointed to Willow, Mai, and two other girls. "You can do the washing in that big tub over there," she said, pointing to a round tub filled with steaming water. She assigned four other girls the task of rinsing.

Then she handed towels to Zenda and three other girls. "You four will be drying," she said. "Thanks!"

Zenda took her place next to the rinsing tub with the other dryers: a tall, slim girl with straight, black hair; a short girl with two brown ponytails; and a girl with short, sandy blond hair. They all looked very friendly. Zenda thought about introducing herself, but found that the words didn't seem to want to come out.

Thankfully, the girl with black hair wasn't as shy. She turned to Zenda. "I'm Kyomi," she said, smiling.

Zenda relaxed and smiled back. "Hi. I'm

Zenda," she said.

One of the rinsers passed a wet dish to Zenda, and she began to dry.

"That's a pretty name," Kyomi replied. "Isn't it amazing here? There are so many interesting people. I met a girl this morning who can turn water into ice just by passing her hand over it. I couldn't believe it."

"Wow," Zenda said, cringing after she said it. Why couldn't she think of an interesting reply?

"I found out at my *harana* that I have aura sight," Kyomi said. "Of course, it's pretty common in my village. Nothing special."

"I have aura sight, too!" Zenda blurted out. "And *kani*. Well, I had *kani* first, but that was before I got my gazing ball. I didn't know if I was going to get to keep my *kani*, or get another gift. Instead, I got to keep both."

Zenda realized she was babbling and blushed. But Kyomi didn't seem to notice.

"Two gifts? Now that really is amazing,"

Kyomi said. "You should come to my cabin after lunch. It's the one closest to the woods. There are a few girls here with aura sight. We're all going to meet."

"That would be great," Zenda said, then suddenly remembered that Alexandra had invited her to a meeting with the girls who had *kani*. "Oh. I'm supposed to do something else. But maybe I can come to the next one?"

"Try and make it!" Kyomi pleaded. "It will be fun! And I want to find out more about your two gifts."

"Okay," Zenda replied. Was this what it was always going to be like, having two gifts? Would she always have to choose one over the other?

After the dishes were done, the girls went their separate ways. Zenda found herself standing in front of the cabin, not sure of what to do about Kyomi. She wanted to go to the meeting about aura sight, but she didn't want to hurt Alexandra's feelings.

Persuaja would know what to do. Zenda grabbed a moonglow flower from outside the cabin door. She walked around the grounds, searching for Persuaja's cabin. She went from cabin to cabin until she reached the smallest one, set off by the others. When she got closer, she saw an open eye carved into the door. Back home, Persuaja had an open eye carved on her front door. This had to be her cabin.

Zenda walked up the steps to the door, which was partly open. She knocked softly, but no one answered. She pushed open the door and stepped inside.

The room looked like a smaller version of Persuaja's home. Silk scarves draped the walls. A long, rectangular table on the right wall held rocks, crystals, and flickering candles. Persuaja and Astrid sat in the center of the room around a small crystal ball on a pedestal. Both had their eyes closed, but Persuaja opened hers as soon as Zenda stepped in.

"Sorry," Zenda said, startled. "I'll come back later."

"Are you sure?" Persuaja asked. Astrid's eyes opened, and she frowned slightly. Zenda noticed a faint green glow around Astrid's body—an aura, for sure—but she had no idea what it meant.

"Sure," Zenda said. "It's not important."

Back in the cabin, Zenda found Alexandra alone, sitting cross-legged on the cot, reading a book. She brightened when she saw Zenda.

"I can't wait to talk about *kani* today," she said. "There's so much I don't know about it."

"I know how you feel," Zenda said, taking the opportunity to gingerly bring up the subject of Kyomi. "I met this really nice girl doing dishes after breakfast. She has aura sight. She and some other girls are meeting after lunch today . . ."

"Oh, you should go!" Alexandra said. "It's good to meet new people. Plus I bet you're anxious to learn more about aura sight. *Kani* must be pretty boring to you by now."

Zenda smiled, grateful for Alexandra's understanding. It was as though she knew just what Zenda was thinking. The realization surprised Zenda. She had been happy enough that she and Alexandra had found a truce; now they seemed to be on the road to becoming friends. It felt good.

"You don't mind?" Zenda asked.

"Of course not," Alexandra said.

At lunch, after she'd finished eating, Zenda found Kyomi at her table in the meal hall.

"Hi," she said shyly.

"Hey, Zenda!" Kyomi cried. She turned to the girls at her table. "This is the girl I was telling you about."

Kyomi pointed to a thin girl with long, white blond hair, and another girl with curly black hair and dark skin. "This is Lana and Devi," she said. "They both have aura sight, too. Let's go back to my cabin now, okay?"

The two girls nodded. Zenda followed them out to Kyomi's cabin. Inside, one of the cots was piled with white silk pillows. Somebody had cut flowers out of delicate paper in pink and blue and had strung them around the cot frame. It looked beautiful.

Zenda was not surprised when Kyomi walked over to the cot. It suited her. Kyomi handed them each a pillow, and they sat on the cabin floor.

Zenda wondered what was going to happen. She didn't know much about aura sight, or how to use it. She knew aura healers could look at the energy field around a person and use it to tell their emotional and physical states. If a person's energy was out of balance or had a troubled aura, plant essences could be prescribed to set the aura right again. It all seemed very complicated to Zenda.

"You guys are as excited as I am," Kyomi began. "I can tell by your auras.

They're all like this bright golden yellow!"

"Really?" Zenda asked, squinting. She didn't see a thing.

"I see it," Lana said in a dreamy voice. "It's faint, but I see it."

Devi shook her head. "I don't see anything," she said. "After my *harana*, I saw auras everywhere. Now I have to really concentrate just to see anything."

"Me too," Zenda said, grateful she wasn't alone. "And when I do see colors, I don't know what they mean. There are so many different shades of each color. How do you tell them apart?"

"Try this," Kyomi suggested. "Take deep breaths. And don't focus your eyes too much. Just sort of . . . gaze."

Zenda took a deep breath. So did Lana and Devi. Zenda tried to relax and look at Kyomi, trying to see something, anything. But she just found herself squinting again.

Nothing. She couldn't see a thing. She

shook her head in frustration.

"Hey, Zenda, that's cool!" Kyomi said.

"What?" Zenda asked, then realized Kyomi was looking at her flower crown. Zenda took it off her head. The flower buds had opened, revealing tiny white roses.

"This happens sometimes," Zenda said. "My *kani* does things I can't control. I thought it was getting better, but I'm not so sure."

"Whatever it is, it's amazing," Kyomi said. "It must be great to have two gifts."

"I guess," Zenda said, but she was starting to worry. She still had a lot of work to do on her *kani*. And it seemed like she would never learn how to use her aura sight.

Zenda left the meeting feeling frustrated and anxious. She went right back to her cabin and took out her journal.

I don't know if I will ever get the hang of my aura sight. And what happened

with the flower crown worries me. I should be more in control of my kani by now. Its almost like . . . I can't do both at once.

Why is it that nothing I try ever comes out exactly right? I don't know how to talk to people. Everything I say comes out wrong. I just really want to be good at my gifts—but it seems like that will never happen. And now I'm getting impatient again, and I know its not good to be impatient. So now what? Maybe I should try to meditate or something. I'm so confused!

Cosmically yours,
Zenda

The Nocti

Zenda spent the rest of the afternoon in the meditation room, trying to clear her mind. Kaveri, the red-haired meditation leader, held a new meditation every two hours. She had good advice for the girls. Zenda tried to do as she was told: When a stray thought entered her mind, she acknowledged it. Then she imagined the thought passing through an open door. That worked for Zenda for a minute or two. The rest of the time, she found herself peering at the other girls under her eyelids, hoping to see signs of auras around them, but she didn't see a thing. She left the meditation cabin feeling more frustrated than when she had arrived.

Camille sensed her mood that night at dinner.

"Maybe you need to relax a little, Zenda," Camille suggested. "We should try to have fun tonight. And tomorrow morning I'm going to go into the woods to look for fiddle-bugs. I was reading today that they make a

47

chirping noise at midnight. Do you want to go with me?"

"That sounds good," Zenda said, relieved. She was probably putting too much pressure on herself. The retreat was supposed to be about relaxing and preparing for school, wasn't it? No one expected her to be an expert at her gifts by the end of Astral Summer.

After breakfast the next morning, Zenda and Camille headed toward the woods.

It seemed to be even darker in there, if that was possible. Zenda shivered.

"How are we supposed to find a bug in here?" Zenda asked. "I can barely see."

"You just need to know where to look," Camille answered. "Fiddlebugs like to live in rotting logs. If we find a rotting log, we should find some fiddlebugs."

"Gross," Zenda said. "Why couldn't they live in a daisy patch or something?"

Camille giggled, and the girls walked along the trail together.

A few minutes later, Zenda saw a young oak that had been most likely struck by lightning. The tree lay in pieces on the ground, surrounded by piles of brown, decaying leaves.

"How about there?" Zenda asked, pointing out the site to Camille.

"Let's try," Camille said. The girls walked off the trail. Now the earth felt soft and spongy under Zenda's feet. Camille approached the fallen tree and knelt down to examine it more closely.

"Here we are," she said finally.

Zenda crouched down to get a better look. Underneath a fallen tree branch crawled several silver bugs that glowed slightly in the dark. Camille closed her eyes and held her hand open, palm up.

Zenda waited silently while Camille sat perfectly still, her hand patiently outstretched. After a few minutes, two of the fiddlebugs crawled onto Camille's hand. She opened her eyes, smiled, and raised her hand up to her face.

"Thank you," she said softly. Then she reached into a cloth pouch tied around her waist and pulled out a small glass jar. She dropped some of the rotting tree bark into the jar, along with some dried, brown leaves. Then she placed her palm next to the rim of the jar, and the bugs crawled inside. Camille screwed a lid onto the jar and stood up.

"Perfect," she said. "That was faster than I thought. Do you want to keep walking?"

"We should get back on the trail," Zenda said a little nervously.

Camille nodded in agreement, and the girls stepped forward. Then Zenda suddenly stopped.

"Did you hear that?" she asked. A soft sound, like a mewing kitten, was coming from somewhere behind them.

"Yes," Camille replied. "It sounds like a baby animal. Maybe it's in trouble."

The soft whimper came again, and the girls turned around and followed the sound.

They traced it to the roots of a nearby oak tree. Zenda and Camille shone the moonglow flowers they were carrying on the roots.

A tiny creature looked up at them with round yellow eyes. It had white fur all over its body, short ears on top of its head, and a long, thin tail.

"It's a nocti," Camille said. "They sleep all year, except when Astral Summer comes."

Zenda knelt down. "It's so cute!" she said. Up close, she could see that one of the animal's thin legs was twisted backward. "I think it's hurt."

Both girls had the same thought. "Willow," they said simultaneously. Their friend could communicate with animals; maybe she could help the nocti.

"Do you think it will come to us?" Zenda asked.

"We should try," Camille said. "If not, we'll bring Willow here."

Camille unhooked her cloth pouch and

handed it to Zenda. Zenda reached out, holding the pouch in a trembling hand.

But the nocti seemed to know that the girls wanted to help it. It cautiously limped inside the pouch. Zenda gently picked it up and cradled it in her hands like a baby.

"Let's go," Zenda said.

Luckily, the girls found Willow in the cabin. Zenda placed the pouch on Willow's cot.

"It's a nocti," Zenda said. "It's hurt."

Willow's eyes widened. She opened the pouch and the nocti crawled out, making a high-pitched whimper. Willow held out her hand and the nocti sniffed it. Then Willow gently began to pet its neck.

"I'm not getting much," Willow said. "I think it is lost. And hurt. It was scared in the woods and wants a safe place to stay."

"Will its leg get better?" Camille asked.

"I think so," Willow said. "We should try to make it comfortable so it can heal."

"What does it eat?" Zenda asked.

"I'm not sure," Willow said. "Let me find out."

Willow began to pet the nocti again until she got her answer. "Ripe duskberries," she announced finally. "They're its favorite, anyway."

Zenda nodded. "I think I saw some growing on the edge of the woods. I'll go get some."

"I'll come with you," Camille said. She placed her fiddlebugs safely in her trunk, and the two girls headed back outside.

They found the duskberries exactly where Zenda had remembered. There was only one problem—the berries were dark green, not the deep purple color they became when ripe.

"They won't ripen until after Astral Summer," Camille said, frowning.

"Maybe I can help," Zenda said. She closed her eyes and placed her hands on the duskberry bush.

First Zenda tried sending a message to the plant, asking the berries to ripen to help the nocti. She opened her eyes, but the berries were still green.

Zenda frowned.

"They're probably sleeping until the sun comes back," Camille guessed.

Until the sun comes back . . . Camille's words gave Zenda an idea. She closed her eyes again. This time, she thought about the sun. The Sun Dancers danced into her head, circling and circling until a wave of bright light poured from them. She imagined the sun's rays bathing her, bathing the duskberry bush . . .

"Zenda, you did it!" Camille cried. Zenda opened her eyes. A cluster of purple duskberries touched her fingers.

Zenda picked as much as she and Camille could hold, and they headed back to the cabin. Willow had managed to make a home for the nocti out of an old fruit crate with a screen on top for a lid. The nocti lay inside, sleeping peacefully against a curled-up cotton shirt. Zenda lifted the lid and placed some of the berries inside. The nocti immediately woke up and walked to the berries, greedily gulping them down.

"Thanks, Zenda," Willow said. "I think he's going to be all right."

"I hope so," Zenda said.

The story of the nocti spread throughout the meal hall at lunchtime. Alexandra insisted that Zenda come to the *kani* meeting that day to tell everyone how she had got the berries to ripen, and Zenda agreed. When her *kani* worked, it felt so good. She got excited about her gift all over again.

Zenda was leaving the meal cabin when Persuaja approached her.

"I heard you had quite an adventure today," she said. "I hope, however, that you did not go into the woods alone."

"Camille was with me," Zenda said. "We were looking for fiddlebugs."

Persuaja nodded. "Of course," she said, smiling slightly. "Zenda, I wanted to apologize for not having time to talk with you yesterday. I hope you understand. Astrid needs my guidance."

"I still need you, too," Zenda blurted out, realizing how childish she sounded as soon as the words came out. She blushed.

"Friends always need each other," Persuaja said gently. "But you have grown so much since we first met, Zenda. I am confident that you can work most things out for yourself. You are stronger than you know. And things did work out, didn't they?"

Zenda thought about it. She had been so worried about hurting Alexandra's feelings by going to Kyomi's meetings. But all she had to do was explain, and Alexandra understood. It wasn't the big problem she had thought it was.

"You're right," Zenda admitted. "But I'm still confused about other things. Like my *kani*. It's sort of messing up again."

Persuaja nodded. "It is your two gifts," she said. "They are struggling to coexist within you. In time, they may both become strong. But if you choose, you may focus on one gift only. Eventually, your other gift will fade."

"Really?" Zenda had never considered this. Could she really give up one gift for another? But what if having two gifts was what made her special? She looked up at Persuaja, confused.

"You will figure things out in time," Persuaja said. She turned to leave, then stopped and turned back to Zenda.

"Make sure you take some time on this retreat to find out who you are, Zenda," she said. "It might be the most important thing you can do."

Before Zenda could ask any questions, Persuaja walked away. Zenda shook her head. Why did Persuaja always have to be so mysterious?

Fallen

I can't believe we have been here for a week! I think everyone is getting used to being here. It feels like home, in a way.

Sophia has covered the walls of our cabin with sound paintings. They are not supposed to make any sound unless you study them, but every once in a while one lets out a strange squeak or a scream. Not all of them are like that, though. My favorite one is a picture of a rain cloud. When you look at it, a musical sound, like falling rain, comes out. It's nice.

Camille has jars of bugs wherever you look. The beetle wakes us in the morning. And the biddlebugs woke us at midnight the first night they were here. Who would think such little bugs could make so much noise! Now Camille keeps them outside, on the steps.

Mai spends almost every hour meditating. I don't know how she does it. I can only do about twenty minutes without starting to itch and twitch. I guess I still need to work on my patience!

Willow says the nocti is getting better. Its leg doesn't look so twisted. Willow lets it out on her cot, but she is afraid to let it loose just yet. She says it isn't ready.

I also figured out what to do about studying my kani and my aura sight. I meet with Alexandra's group one day, and with Kyomi, Lana, and Devi the next. Kyomi is so nice! I am glad I got to know her. Maybe I won't be so shy about meeting new people in the future.

In a few days everyone is gathering in the center circle to have a bonfire and a dance. Some of the girls here brought drums from home, so it should be really amazing. I can't wait! I haven't danced in weeks.

I saw Persuaja a couple of days ago. She gave me some tips on how crystals can be used to strengthen aura sight, but I haven't tried them out yet. Astrid is with her all the time! It's funny, she used to be Alexandra's shadow, and now she's Persuaja's. Maybe she doesn't like being in the spotlight.

I'd better go! There's a sela class in a few minutes.

Cosmically yours,
Zenda

Zenda closed her journal and swung off the bed. Sophia came out of the bathroom, holding a bunch of freshly cleaned paint-brushes.

"Hey, Zen," she said. "Do you want to do something? Believe it or not, I don't feel like painting anymore today."

"I'm going to *sela* class," Zenda said. "Want to come?"

Sophia shrugged. "Why not?"

When the girls arrived at the *sela* cabin, they found that Miyo, the instructor, had set up short, round tree stumps all around the room. Their tops had been sanded smoothly, so that they were perfectly level. Miyo stood in front of the room, wearing loose blue pants and a sleeveless white top.

"We are going to work on balance today," Miyo instructed. "Find a stump that feels good. We are about to begin."

Zenda and Sophia exchanged glances and took their places in front of two neighboring tree stumps. Zenda looked around at the other girls. She recognized a few of the girls, but the only other girl there from their village was Astrid, who had taken her place in front of a stump in the corner.

At the front of the room, Miyo stood on top of one of the stumps.

"Please step up and find your balance," she said. "We are going to try the sunflower pose today."

Zenda carefully stepped up onto her tree stump. The stump felt solid underneath her, and there was plenty of room for her feet.

This shouldn't be too hard, she thought.

Miyo slowly moved into the sunflower pose: both arms raised, palms touching, the right leg lifted with the foot resting against the left knee. Zenda put her arms in position and then slowly lifted her leg. She closed her eyes.

The pose was challenging, but Zenda found her balance. She remembered to breathe deeply.

"Forget that you are standing on the tree stump," Miyo told them. "Imagine roots growing from the bottom of your left foot, roots growing deep into the ground."

Zenda visualized the roots, just as Miyo said, and she found she felt stronger.

"Good, good," Miyo was saying. "Nice job, Zenda."

Zenda opened her eyes and smiled back at her teacher. She was about to close her eyes again when she felt a strange feeling on the back of her neck—as though someone was watching her. She craned her neck. Sure enough, Astrid was staring right at her, a dark look on her face.

Startled, Zenda dropped the pose for a second.

That's strange, she thought. She took another deep breath and moved into the pose again. She felt strong, grounded . . .

Suddenly, the tree stump began to rock beneath Zenda's foot. It felt to Zenda like

64

someone was pushing up the stump from underneath. Zenda lost her balance and fell. Her ankle twisted painfully as she hit the floor.

"*Ow!*" Zenda cried. The girls crowded around her, and Miyo pushed her way through.

"You're hurt," she said. She turned to Sophia. "Go find Sabra."

Sophia dashed out and returned a few minutes later with Sabra.

"I'm not sure what happened," Zenda said. "It felt like somebody moved the tree stump underneath me."

Miyo shook her head. "It is odd," she said. "I saw the stump move. But they're all level, and very sturdy. I'm sorry, Zenda."

"It's okay," she said. Then she groaned as Sabra lifted up her ankle.

"It's a bad sprain," Sabra said. "You'll have to stay off of it for a few days."

"What do you mean, stay off of it?"

Zenda asked.

"I mean, you'll need to stay in bed for a while," Sabra said, smiling. "Don't worry. We'll make sure you have lots of visitors. It'll be fun—like a sleepover that never ends."

Zenda held back tears. It didn't sound fun at all. She hated being stuck in bed. Celine arrived and she and Sabra carried Zenda back to her cabin.

Word spread around the cabins about Zenda's accident, and soon she was surrounded by her friends in her cot. Sabra came back with a large chunk of ice wrapped in cloth.

"I'll come by again later with an herbal compress," she said. "You'll be out of this bed in no time."

Sabra left, and Sophia, Camille, Willow, and Alexandra gathered closer.

"Zenda, I'm so sorry!" Camille said.

"It's my own fault," Zenda said. "I'm so clumsy!"

"I don't know," Sophia said. "I saw the

way Astrid was looking at you."

"What are you saying?" Alexandra asked defensively. She and Astrid were still friends, Zenda knew.

Sophia shrugged. "I don't know," she said. "Astrid has weird powers, right? Maybe she made Zenda fall."

"That's ridiculous," Alexandra said, her face growing dark. "Astrid wouldn't hurt anybody. I know her better than you."

"Of course," Zenda said. "I just fell. That's all."

At that moment the door opened, and Astrid came into the room. She quickly walked to her cot without looking at anyone and picked up a book.

Sophia glared at her. "Astrid, it's terrible what happened to Zenda, isn't it?"

Astrid flushed bright red. "Yes," she said quickly. Then she looked down at the pages of the book, avoiding Sophia's gaze.

Outside, the supper chimes rang.

"All right," Zenda said. "Who wants to bring me dinner? I'm really hungry. Spraining your ankle is hard work."

Camille and Willow laughed. Sophia and Alexandra were still looking at each other with unsure expressions.

Zenda laughed, but underneath it, she felt uneasy. *Something* strange had happened in *sela* class. But what?

Zenda wasn't sure. But she was going to find out.

Visions

I am in a bad mood.

I can't help it. I know I have only been stuck in bed for three days, but it feels like weeks and weeks. Sabra won't let me walk any farther than the bathroom. She makes me keep an herbal compress on my ankle all the time. It smells like rotten potatoes!

Camille stays with me sometimes, and so do Sophia and Willow. But everyone is busy most of the time. The only company I have are Camille's bugs and the nocti. Now I know how it feels. I might as well be stuck in the fruit crate with it!

It sounds like someone is coming. I'm

*going to go. But I know I'll be writing
again soon. What else do I have to do?*

Cosmically yours,
Zenda

All of the girls from the cabin came
through the door. Camille held a tray of hot
food.

"Supper time, Zenda!" she announced.

Zenda looked down at the plate of pasta
and vegetables and hunk of chewy bread that
Camille set down in front of her.

"Thanks," she said, lazily picking up her
fork. She wasn't particularly hungry, but she
thought she might as well eat.

Around her, Zenda noticed that the
other girls were quickly changing their clothes

and brushing their hair.

"What's going on?" she asked.

"It's the bonfire tonight," Camille said. "I almost forgot. Sabra said you can go if you want."

Zenda brightened. "Really?"

Camille nodded. "She and Celine will carry you there. She said no dancing. But you can still have fun!"

Zenda's mood dipped once again. She suddenly felt grumpier than ever. What fun would the bonfire be if she couldn't dance? And she hated the idea of being carried, like some kind of baby.

"I'm going to stay here," she said.

"Zenda, no!" Camille cried. "Please come."

But Zenda just felt more stubborn with each minute. "I'll be fine," she said. "You can tell me all about it when it's over."

Camille frowned. "I'll come back early," she said.

"Don't worry about me," Zenda sighed.

A half an hour later, the cabin was empty once again. Zenda immediately regretted her decision, but it was too late. In the distance, she could hear the sound of drums pounding and girls laughing. She sank back on her pillows.

She didn't feel like reading or writing in her journal. She sat up and hobbled over to the nocti's crate. She lifted the lid and cradled the furry little animal in her palm. His leg looked straight and healthy now.

"You'll be all better soon," she said, stroking his fur. "Good for you. I'll probably be stuck in this cabin forever!"

As soon as Zenda said the words out loud, she laughed. Something dark and gloomy broke inside her. How sad and pathetic she sounded! And all because of a sprained ankle.

Zenda put the nocti back in its crate and replaced the lid.

"I've got to make the best of this," she

said with newfound confidence. "There's got to be something I can do."

Then Zenda remembered something Kaveri had taught them during a meditation class. She had told the girls about positive visualization: In a meditative state, they could visualize things they wanted, really picture them happening.

"All action starts with vision," Kaveri said. "It's the first step."

It was worth a try. Zenda couldn't sit with her legs crossed, so she sat on the edge of her bed. She closed her eyes and began to slow down her breathing. Then she slowly counted backward, starting with ten. She pictured the numbers in her mind. Ten . . . nine . . . eight . . . When she reached one, Zenda imagined a blank screen in her mind. Then she conjured up a picture of herself. What was the most positive thing she could imagine? She saw herself standing on two feet, walking across the room. No, running across a field. Her legs felt strong.

Zenda smiled. This felt kind of fun.

While I'm at it, I might as well try visualizing some more, she thought.

She changed the scene in her mind. Now she stood in the meal hall. Her dress was perfect—not a wrinkle or a stain. Her curly hair fell neatly on her shoulders, not in a tangled mess. Zenda was talking to girls she didn't know, making them laugh, holding their attention.

More, Zenda told herself. *Why not more?*

In the next image, every girl in the room was glowing with a different colored aura. Zenda walked gracefully around the room, identifying each girl's aura one by one as they oohed and aahed in response.

Zenda opened her eyes and discovered she was smiling. She liked the way she looked in her visualization: cool, confident, and an expert aura reader . . . a lot like Kyomi, Zenda realized.

Zenda pondered this for a minute. Her *kani* had not appeared anywhere in her vision. Did that mean that she didn't want her *kani* anymore? Had she already made her choice, deep down? The thought troubled her.

"Well, I *think* it was a positive visualization," she said out loud. "Right, nocti?"

Zenda turned to the fruit crate. Then she gasped.

The lid had been pushed to the side. Zenda hopped over to the crate. The nocti was gone!

Frantic, Zenda dropped to her knees. She looked under every cot. She hopped to the bathroom and searched every corner. Then, reluctantly, she turned to the front door.

The door was opened a crack. A small crack, but large enough for a nocti to get through.

Zenda looked down at her ankle. It was throbbing, but she had no choice. Gritting her teeth, she limped out the door into the night.

After Midnight

Zenda picked up a handful of moonglow flowers and walked to the back of the cabin, trying not to put too much pressure on her ankle. Each step hurt. Luckily, the woods were right behind her. She could enter fairly quickly, without being seen.

"Here, nocti," she whispered. "Please come back. Willow needs to make sure you're okay to be out on your own."

Why are you so careless sometimes? she scolded herself. *I bet nothing like this happens to Kyomi.*

Zenda walked deeper into the woods, but there was no sign of the little creature. She started to head back to the trail, but went several yards without reaching it.

You're lost, Zenda realized. She tried not to panic. The trail had to be around somewhere. Zenda traced her steps.

Zenda had no idea how long it took her to find the trail again. Looking back, she guessed it must have been several hours.

When she finally found the path, exhausted and in tears, she sank against an old oak tree.

She heard a tiny cry above her and looked up. The nocti sat on a low tree branch. Before she could react, it jumped onto her shoulder. Zenda quickly grabbed it, sighing gratefully.

The party had to be winding down by now, Zenda knew. People would be looking for her. She hoped they would understand. After all, she had been through worse before. Zenda started back down the trail.

Then she heard another noise.

Breee! Breee! Breee!

The fiddlebugs, Zenda realized. They sounded just as loud as they had in the cabin that first night Camille brought them back, waking everyone up at midnight.

Midnight . . . the word sent a chill through Zenda's body. What had Persuaja said? Something about not going into the woods after midnight, when the rendulla flower blooms.

She half walked, half ran down the path, ignoring her hurt ankle. She had to get back to the cabin — fast.

As Zenda hurried, she noticed an odd smell in the air. It was thick and sweet and permeated the woods quite quickly. In spite of herself, she stopped.

She breathed deeply, inhaling the scent. Without even thinking about it, she turned, following the smell. There, just off the trail, a tall flower stem rose up from behind a rock. Two flowers bloomed at the top of the stem: one black, and one red.

Don't go near it, a voice inside her warned. But Zenda moved in closer, compelled by the scent. The nocti squeaked and scurried off her shoulder. Zenda didn't even notice.

Suddenly, her body felt tingly. She felt her eyes closing.

The next thing she knew, Zenda was

waking up. She apparently had been sleeping on the trail. The strange smell was gone. The moonglow flowers lay on the dirt next to her, all of their light faded. Zenda looked behind the rock, but the two flower buds were closed tightly. And the nocti was nowhere in sight.

Zenda had a terrible feeling. She had encountered some strange flowers before, and bad things had happened. Like an orchid that made your emotions go out of control. And a flower that sent you to another dimension.

The flower with the twin buds, she was sure, was the endangered rendulla flower. She had no idea what happened when one encountered a rendulla after midnight. She stood up and brushed the dirt off of her. She *seemed* fine.

If the rendulla flower had caused something strange to happen, there was only one way to find out. She walked back down the trail.

Zenda Here
and There

It wasn't easy getting back to the cabin without the moonglow flowers. Zenda took careful steps, being sure to stay on the trail. Thoughts swirled in her mind as she walked. How long had she been gone? What would Persuaja say? After all this, she didn't even have the nocti. Zenda's eyes filled with tears.

As she reached the village, Zenda looked down at herself. Her white dress was streaked with dirt. She put a hand to her hair, which felt like a tangled mess. She pulled out a few dried leaves. She took a deep breath. It didn't matter what she looked like. She had to face the others, no matter what. She slowly walked toward her cabin.

A few feet away, she heard loud, animated voices. Were they talking about her? It couldn't hurt to know what she was going to be facing. Zenda quietly stepped under one of the cabin windows and listened.

"I can't believe you went into the woods by yourself! You should have come and got me." That was Camille. But who was she talking to? Had someone gone into the woods behind her?

Then Zenda heard Willow's voice. "How did you find the nocti, Zenda?"

Zenda panicked. Had Willow seen her? She looked around. No one was outside. Curious, she peered into the window.

Her friends were gathered around Zenda's cot: Camille, Willow, Sophia, Alexandra, Mai, and Gena. Only Astrid was missing. Sitting on the cot, in a clean white dress, her reddish-gold hair neatly brushed, was Zenda!

Outside the window, Zenda let out a small scream. She quickly put her hand over her mouth and ducked under the window, her heart pounding wildly.

"What was that?" Sophia asked inside.

A voice answered her—a voice Zenda knew without a doubt was her own voice.

"Maybe it was an owl," the Zenda inside

the cabin said. "I saw one in the woods. Its claws were long and sharp. That's when I knew I had to find the nocti, no matter what. If I hadn't, I'm sure the owl would have eaten the poor nocti for lunch."

"You're so brave, Zenda!" Zenda heard Gena say.

"It wasn't brave, really," the other Zenda replied. "I did what I had to do."

Zenda's mind raced. Was this some kind of dream? It couldn't really be another her in there, could it? It must be somebody who looked like her, or sounded like her. She was tired. She must have seen things wrong. She cautiously looked in the window once more.

The girl on the cot was stroking the nocti, telling the story of how she had gone into the woods to save it. The other girls listened, entranced. She was definitely a better storyteller than Zenda. But otherwise, the girl looked just like herself. Only cleaner, maybe.

Zenda sank under the window again.

Looking at the other Zenda was difficult. It was like she was outside of her own body.

Is that what had happened? Was she some kind of spirit, floating outside herself? Zenda pinched her arm to be sure. It hurt. She pressed her hand against the cabin. It felt solid. No, she was real.

But clearly, so was the other Zenda.

Think, Zenda, think! She told herself. It had to have something to do with the rendulla flower. She had smelled the flower, and now there were two of her. It had to be related.

Part of her wanted to go in the cabin right then and confront the other Zenda, but she held back. That could be dangerous. She needed more information first.

Sometimes it takes more courage to ask for help than to act alone. Her ninth musing came to mind. It was a good one. Zenda knew she could not handle this herself.

But one person could. As quickly as she could, she headed toward Persuaja's cabin.

The Astral
Double

The grounds were quiet as Zenda headed to the cabin with the open eye carved into the door. She stepped up to the door, ready to knock. But a small sign hung there, written in Persuaja's ornate script: *Do not disturb.*

Zenda hesitated. This was an emergency, certainly. Persuaja wouldn't mind being disturbed for that, would she? Zenda wasn't sure.

Zenda moved away from the door and looked in the front window. Sheer purple curtains hung there, but Zenda could see through the thin space where the curtains met.

Persuaja and Astrid sat in the middle of the room again, this time on thick purple cushions. They both looked like they were meditating. Zenda was surprised to realize that she could see both of their auras clearly. Persuaja's was a calm, light blue, and Astrid's was soft pink.

Zenda had second thoughts about

telling Persuaja. Hadn't Persuaja said that Zenda was strong enough to handle things by herself?

In addition, a little voice in Zenda's head reminded her that going into the woods after midnight had been strictly forbidden. Would Persuaja send her home? She couldn't face that kind of embarrassment again. It was just like when she broke her gazing ball.

Zenda walked to the meal hall, keeping in the shadows. When she arrived, all the girls were inside. She didn't want to risk being seen through the wide windows, so she found a clump of rosebushes next to the meal hall and hid behind them.

After what seemed like hours, girls started to exit the meal hall. Zenda cringed to see the other Zenda walk out with Kyomi, Lana, and Devi. The girls stopped in front of the hall, and then the other Zenda waved and headed toward the meditation hall. Zenda noticed, curiously, that her double wasn't limping.

The double definitely existed, there was no doubt about that. Zenda was burning with curiosity. Was this girl really a duplicate of herself? She wanted to know more.

Zenda carefully left her hiding place and followed her double from a distance. The other Zenda entered the meditation cabin. Zenda waited a few moments for the meditation to begin. Then she crept up to the cabin window and looked inside.

Her double sat on a silk cushion among the other meditating girls. Zenda saw Mai there as well. Most of the girls twitched, stretched out legs and arms, or opened their eyes during the meditation. Mai was perfectly still, and to Zenda's amazement, so was her double. Her face was a perfect picture of stillness.

Why can my double meditate, but I can't? Zenda wondered. Something very strange was going on.

Then she felt a tap on her shoulder, and

jumped. She turned to see Kyomi staring at her quizzically.

"Why so jumpy?" she asked. Kyomi squinted. "Your aura is flaring on and off. Something's wrong."

"N-no, everything's fine," Zenda stammered. What else could Kyomi tell from her aura?

"Maybe we should go meditate," Kyomi said. "I thought that's where you were going."

Zenda quickly steered Kyomi away from the cabin. "This morning's session is canceled," she lied. "Kaveri left a note."

"Oh," Kyomi said uncertainly. She looked at Zenda again. "You look different than you did at breakfast. Weren't you wearing different clothes?"

"I, uh, spilled something at breakfast," Zenda said. "Listen, I'm just tired. I'm going to go lie down."

Kyomi nodded. "But you're still coming to my cabin for the meeting, right?" she asked.

"Of course," Zenda said. Kyomi walked away, casting suspicious glances behind her.

Zenda sighed with relief and rested against a nearby tree. That was a close call. If she didn't do something soon, everyone at the retreat would know about her double. She definitely needed help.

She wanted Camille.

Zenda checked the cabin first. She found Camille inside, by herself. Zenda put her face to the open window and called out, "Camille!" in an anxious whisper.

"Zenda?" Camille turned around. "What are you doing at the window?"

"We need to talk," Zenda said.

Camille came out of the cabin, a puzzled look on her face.

"I thought you went off with Kyomi," she said. "And you're wearing different clothes. Is everything all right?"

"I'll tell you everything," Zenda said. "But we've got to get out of here."

Camille followed Zenda without a word. Zenda led her to the edge of the woods, and sat down behind a thick old oak.

"Something happened in the woods last night," Zenda began.

"I know," Camille said. "You told us."

Zenda shook her head. "That wasn't me," she said, struggling to explain. "I mean, she *is* me, maybe. But she's *another* me."

Camille's brown eyes looked worried. "Zenda, what are you talking about?"

"I went into the woods last night," Zenda said. "I got lost. I found the nocti. But then the fiddlebugs chirped, and I knew it was midnight. Then I smelled something, and I found this flower. I think it was a rendulla."

A look of understanding dawned on Camille's face. "Oh, Zen! Persuaja said—"

Zenda nodded. "I know. I think something happened. When I smelled the flower, I fell asleep. Then I got back to the cabin, but I was already there. I mean, there was another *me* there, talking to you."

Camille put a hand over her mouth, horrified. "You mean, there are two of you?"

Zenda nodded again.

Camille shook her head, dazed. "No. It can't be. That was you in there. Maybe you're seeing things. Or your memory got messed up or something."

Zenda stood up. "I'll prove it to you," she said. She led Camille to Kyomi's cabin. The other Zenda should be there by now, for the aura sight meeting. Zenda put her finger to her lips when they reached the side window. She motioned for Camille to look inside with her.

Inside, the other Zenda was sitting on the floor in a circle with Kyomi, Lana, and Devi.

"You've got a beautiful orange aura today, Devi," the other Zenda was saying. She closed her eyes. "You're happy about something, aren't you?"

94

Devi clapped her hands. "You're right!"

Camille gasped and leaned back against the cabin, a shocked look on her face.

"How do we know you're the real Zenda?"

Alexandra walked up behind them. For a second, Zenda flashed back to her days at school last year. Was Alexandra going to tell everyone what had happened?

"Don't worry," Alexandra said, as if she had read Zenda's mind. "I heard you and Camille talking by the cabin. I want to help. But first, we need to make sure you're the real Zenda."

"What do you mean?" Camille asked.

"Maybe *she's* the double, and the Zenda inside the cabin is the real Zenda," Alexandra said.

Zenda thought. She had to convince her friends. She searched her mind for something that would work. "Camille's middle name is Penelope," she said finally.

Camille cringed.

"I didn't know that," Alexandra said.

"It's true," Camille admitted. "I hate it. Zenda is the only person I've ever told."

"So do you believe me now?" Zenda asked.

Alexandra paused, thinking. "You're the real Zenda, all right," she said finally. "Okay, first we need to find a place where you won't be seen," Alexandra said. "There's an old equipment shed down by the stream. I've been going there to read in the afternoons. No one has seen me yet."

"Let's go," Zenda said.

The path to the stream was lit with moonglow flowers growing on either side. Alexandra and Camille flanked Zenda as they walked. They managed to get to the shed, a small, wooden building, without being seen. Alexandra opened the door, and they stepped inside.

Shovels, rakes, and brooms hung from the walls of the square room. Spiderwebs hung in the corners, reminding Zenda faintly of the silk scarves on Persuaja's walls. Alexandra had set up the space for herself with a thick pillow on the floor, surrounded by jars of moonglow flowers and a stack of books.

The girls settled on the floor while Alexandra searched for a book in the stack.

"Here it is," she said. The green cover was stamped in gold with the title *Endangered Plants of Azureblue.*

"The first time Persuaja mentioned the rendulla flower, I was so curious that I wanted to learn more about it," Alexandra began. "I finally found a page on it in this book. Here's what it says:

"The rendulla flower still grows wild in certain protected wooded areas in the west. Many years ago, the flower was almost harvested to extinction by healers looking for ways to use the flower's peculiar properties for good.

"The flower blooms after midnight,

only during *Astral Summer. If anyone smells the flower's scent in bloom, the rendulla flower will create a duplicate of that person—what has come to be called an astral double. The duplicate seems to take on the idealized traits of the original subject. In other words, the duplicate acts and looks the way the subject wishes he or she acted or looked.*"

Zenda tried to fathom this. "So the double is me, but she's *not* me?"

"She's what you wish you could be," Alexandra said. "The book goes on to explain that in older times, the original person and the astral double would have to live together, like sisters or brothers or something. But then they found a cure."

Alexandra turned the book to them so they could read the page. "There are a few ingredients, but I think we can get them all in the woods here," she said. "It might take some time, though."

"How long?" Zenda asked. The idea of her double walking around made her nervous.

"You can stay here," Alexandra said confidently. "No one will find you. We'll make the potion, and you'll be back to normal again. And nobody has to know."

Zenda turned to Camille. "What do you think?"

Her friend looked dazed. "Maybe we should tell Persuaja," she said. "This is an awfully big thing to keep secret."

"I thought about that," Zenda said. "But Persuaja is busy with Astrid. And I don't want to get in trouble for going near the rendulla flower after midnight. What if they make me leave the retreat?"

"We don't need Persuaja," Alexandra said firmly. "This is going to be easy."

"Okay," Zenda said. "Let's make that potion."

The Other
Zenda

Zenda waited, nervously tapping her foot in the shed as Alexandra and Camille went out to find the ingredients for the potion. They both came back about an hour later, each carrying a small cloth sack.

Alexandra opened her sack on the floor and took out the contents. "One dandelion root," she said. "And some birch bark."

"And I've got the grouseflower buds," Camille said, taking some pale blue flower buds from her sack. Then she took out a smooth, brown rock. "And one river stone."

"Great!" Zenda said. "So do we just mix this stuff together?"

Alexandra and Camille exchanged worried glances.

"Not just yet," Alexandra said. "We still need one more ingredient."

"It's the lifewort leaves," Camille said. "We couldn't find any."

Zenda got a bad feeling. "What do you mean?"

"There aren't any growing around here," Alexandra said. "But we're going to ask around and see if anyone brought some from home. Sabra might have some in her healing kit.

"We'll be careful," Alexandra continued. "Stop worrying, Zenda. We'll make the potion before you know it. Everything's going to be fine."

But even Alexandra didn't sound as confident as usual. In the distance, the lunch chimes rang.

"So what now?" Zenda asked.

"Try and stay hidden," Alexandra said. "Camille and I will try to find some lifewort leaves. We'll come back as soon as we find some."

Camille looked worried. "Are you going to be okay, Zenda?"

Zenda nodded. "I think so," she said. "But could you please bring me some lunch? I could eat a cactus!"

The afternoon passed slowly. Camille

stayed and talked to Zenda for a while after lunch, but then left to go look for lifewort leaves. Zenda soon became restless. And the idea that her double was out there doing things that people thought *she* was doing—that really bothered her.

Alexandra came to visit right before supper, carrying extra pillows and blankets and a change of clothes.

"What's all this stuff?" Zenda asked suspiciously.

"Don't panic," Alexandra said. "One of the girls said she saw some lifewort growing on the path that leads into the retreat. Camille and I are going to look in the morning."

"In the morning?" Zenda cried. "You mean I have to stay here all night?"

"Lifewort leaves have to be picked in the morning, or they're not as potent," Alexandra said. "That's what the book says. Camille and I will go as early as we can. You'll be back to normal before breakfast."

"This is crazy," Zenda said. "What if the double does something dangerous? What if she hurts somebody?"

"She's not like that," Alexandra said. "I mean, she's not an *evil* you or anything. She's like you only . . . different."

"How different?" Zenda asked.

"It's like the other Zenda is really popular. Everyone wants to be around her. She's fun."

Zenda felt suddenly hurt, and it must have shown on her face. Alexandra quickly tried to cushion her statement. "That's not what I mean," she said. "Everyone likes the real you, too. But your double is more . . . outgoing, I guess. She just puts herself out there."

"Don't people wonder why I've suddenly changed?" Zenda asked.

Alexandra shrugged. "They probably think you've just warmed up. You know, come out of your shell."

The conversation with Alexandra made Zenda feel uneasy. When the supper bell chimed, Zenda decided to venture out of her hiding place. She had to see her double in action.

Everyone was inside the meal hall when Zenda approached. This time, she decided to risk looking in one of the large windows. Zenda saw the other Zenda sitting with Kyomi and her friends a few windows down. Zenda walked to the other window, straining to listen.

"If I give up my *kani*, I can concentrate on my aura sight," the Zenda double said. "It makes sense. Why do two things only half as well, when I can do one thing really well?"

"That's great, Zenda," Kyomi enthused. "I think you'll make a wonderful aura healer."

"I hope so," the other Zenda said.

"Can we do more aura practice tonight?" Lana asked.

"I was thinking," the double said.

"Maybe we should do something fun. How about a bardic circle? I bet we could get the other girls to do it."

Zenda had often seen bardic circles in her own village. Each person in the village contributed something—a song, a poem, a dance, a story. Zenda had always been too shy to participate, but she loved to watch.

"That's an amazing idea!" Kyomi said. She turned to the table next to her. "Hey, Zenda thinks we should do a bardic circle tonight. What do you think?"

The idea quickly spread around the room, and the girls began to talk excitedly. A girl Zenda didn't recognize walked up to her double.

"Great idea, Zenda," said the girl. "You are so much fun!"

"Thanks," the double replied. Unlike the real Zenda, she didn't blush or look down at her plate awkwardly.

The girls began to take their trays to the kitchen. Zenda knew she had to get back to her hiding place before Camille arrived with her supper. She had sprinted there halfway when she realized her ankle seemed to be all better.

"That's one thing down," Zenda muttered. "Now I've just got to get rid of the other me."

Camille arrived a few minutes later with a tray of bean curd and vegetables that smelled exotic and spicy. Zenda hungrily ate the food while she and she talked.

"I hear my double is pretty popular," Zenda said.

Camille shuddered slightly. "I haven't gone near her. Too creepy," Camille said.

"Hasn't anybody noticed?" Zenda asked. "I mean, we're almost always together."

Camille sighed. "Everybody likes being around your double, Zenda," she said. "I think they're glad I'm out of the way."

"Don't say that!" Zenda cried. "You're my best friend. I don't care what my double does. I'll always be your friend."

Camille smiled. "I know," she said. "It's just hard."

Zenda chewed her lower lip, deep in thought. "I don't get it," she said. "My double is supposed to be the me I really want to be, right? So does that mean I want to be popular? I mean, I've thought about being more outgoing, like she is, you know? More confident. But she seems to be taking off in her own direction or something."

Camille's eyes widened. "Maybe the double starts out like you and then changes," she said. "Takes on a life of her own."

"Or maybe she'll take over *my* life," Zenda said grimly. Wasn't that what she was doing already?

"Maybe we should tell Persuaja," Camille said.

"Try to find the lifewort tomorrow," Zenda said. "If you can't, I'll tell Persuaja, okay?"

"Okay," Camille said.

A bug chirped in Camille's pocket, and Zenda knew it was eight o'clock.

"You'd better get to the bardic circle," Zenda said. "You don't want anybody to wonder where you are."

"Right," Camille said. "I hate to leave you, Zen."

"Don't worry about me," Zenda said. "I'll just go to sleep."

Zenda watched Camille go. She didn't want her friend to worry about her, but Zenda had other plans. She waited a few minutes, then headed out to the bardic circle. She had to see what this double of hers was like. Was she really as fun and popular as Alexandra and Camille had said?

Zenda left the equipment shed and headed for the center circle, staying in the shadows. A large circle of girls had gathered there, sitting around a small fire.

"I've got something!" someone exclaimed.

Zenda froze. Her double had jumped to her feet, smiling brightly. Zenda scurried behind a hickory tree and held her breath. What was her double going to do?

"I wrote a poem for tonight," the double announced. "I call it, 'A-muse-ing.' "

Then she began the poem, speaking in a rhythmic voice:

"Thirteen musings.
Words to live by.

Don't do this. But do that.
No. Do that instead!
Ow! My poor head.
I'll do my best.
But I'm only thirteen.
So don't expect miracles, okay?

Thirteen musings.
Swirling in my head.
Most of the time,

110

I
    am
        not
           amused!"

The other Zenda took a little bow. Everyone clapped and laughed.

The real Zenda sat behind her tree, a slow funk coming over her. The double's poem was pretty funny. Zenda felt that way about her musings sometimes. But she would have never been able to express her feelings like that—not in public, anyway. Sure, she wrote in her journal. But she had never written poetry like that. And she couldn't imagine reading it in front of everyone.

Zenda stomped back to her hiding place.

Maybe I should just stay here forever, she thought gloomily. *And let my double go back to the village. I bet everyone would like that!*

Face to Face

Zenda's gloom deepened as she fell into a fitful sleep. A few hours later, a shrill scream woke her.

A chorus of girls began to shout for help. Zenda knew she was supposed to stay hidden, but she couldn't sit here, wondering what was going on. She grabbed a handful of moonglow flowers and ran outside in her bare feet.

A crowd had formed in front of Kyomi's cabin. Zenda found a place behind a nearby tree. Sabra and Celine were running into the cabin. Persuaja walked behind them.

Zenda saw Alexandra looking around with sharp eyes. *She must be worried that I might show up*, Zenda realized. She stepped out briefly from behind the tree and motioned to Alexandra. The tall girl nodded and ran over.

"Kyomi's been bitten by something," Alexandra reported. "Some kind of bug. Her leg is swelling up. Sabra's trying to figure out what's wrong. I'm going to go back to Kyomi's cabin and see what else I can find out."

"Wait!" Zenda said. "Did you find the lifewort leaves?"

"No luck," Alexandra said, distracted. "But don't worry. Something will turn up."

Alexandra walked away, and Zenda's mind raced as she thought about what to do. Things had gone too far. She wanted to tell Persuaja—but she couldn't now. Things were too crazy.

Zenda watched as Sabra came out of the cabin and walked toward Persuaja. The two walked to the side, and Zenda saw that they were coming toward her tree. She crouched down, trying to make herself as small as possible.

She heard their conversation clearly.

"It's a snipe bug bite," Sabra said. "We've never had a snipe bite out here before. I'm not prepared for it. She needs a poultice of beartree sap to stop the swelling," she explained. "But we don't have any."

Persuaja looked thoughtful. "Send Celine to the nearest village," she said. "In the

114

meantime, we will search the woods for beartrees."

"But the trees are in hibernation," Sabra protested. "We won't be able to get any sap from them."

"We can try," Persuaja said, and something in her voice gave Zenda a chill. It was as though her words had taken shape and were reaching around the tree, trying to touch Zenda. Did Persuaja know she was there?

"I'll tell Celine," Sabra said. "In the meantime, I've got some aloe gel. That should help a little."

Persuaja and Sabra left. Alexandra came and found Zenda again. "Persuaja is rounding up those of us with *kani*," she said. "We're going into the woods to find a beartree."

Behind Alexandra, Zenda saw her double reach the group. Sophia ran up to her.

"Zenda, good thing you're here!" she said. "Persuaja needs girls with *kani* to go into the woods to look for a plant to help Kyomi."

The double's eyes widened. "But I'm doing aura sight now," she said.

Sophia looked puzzled. "But you still can do *kani*, right?"

"I can," the double said. "But it's not what I want to do anymore. I'm sure the other girls can handle it."

Sophia scowled, and Zenda felt a pang of annoyance. Was this really her double? She didn't like her very much right now.

Alexandra raised an eyebrow. "Wow, Zenda. You're not very nice."

"That's not me," Zenda protested. "Listen, I'll follow you. I can always pretend to be my double. I won't let Kyomi stay hurt."

Persuaja was leading the girls with *kani* toward the woods. Alexandra ran to catch up to them. Zenda followed behind, hoping not to be seen.

The group did not go far before Persuaja stopped. She pointed to a young, thin tree with narrow, light-green leaves.

"That is a beartree," she said.

Zenda recognized it. She knew the tree got its name because bears loved to eat the sweet sap that flowed inside its branches. But beartrees always went into hibernation during the Astral Summer. No sap flowed through its branches now.

"I need you girls to try to coax the tree out of hibernation," Persuaja said. "Get the sap flowing. Perhaps if you all work together, you can do it."

Zenda held back. She might as well let the other girls try. She didn't want to risk revealing her secret yet.

The girls circled the beartree, each resting her hands on the branches. Zenda watched as they closed their eyes. After a few minutes, they began to open them. They looked disappointed.

"I don't feel anything," Alexandra said. Then she raised her voice pointedly. "It's too bad Zenda isn't here."

Zenda sighed. She had to help Kyomi. At least her double was nowhere in sight. She could fool everyone for a few more hours, surely. She stepped out from her hiding place and walked up to the group. "Hi," she said shyly.

Persuaja raised an eyebrow. "I thought you weren't coming, Zenda," she said.

"I changed my mind," Zenda said quickly. "I want to help. We can all try together."

Zenda joined the circle of girls. Like them, she rested her hands on the tree and closed her eyes. The tree felt cold and still.

"Ask the tree to wake up," Zenda whispered. "Imagine the sap rising from its roots."

Zenda imagined just that, and she hoped the other girls were doing the same. Nothing happened for a few seconds, but then, slowly, Zenda felt warmth beneath her fingers. Then a hum. She opened her eyes. "It's working," she said. "I can feel it."

The other girls murmured in wonder as they felt the sap rising under their fingers.

When Zenda felt the time was right, she asked the tree for permission to take some of its branches. She received a warm feeling in response. Zenda sharply broke off three branches and handed them to Persuaja.

"Is this enough?" she asked.

Persuaja's dark eyes glittered. "More than enough. Well done."

At that moment, Zenda heard someone crashing through the brush. Sophia appeared, dragging the Zenda double behind her.

"I made Zenda come," Sophia explained, looking at Persuaja and Zenda. Then she stopped. Sophia looked back from Zenda to her double. "No way. There are two of you!"

The other girls shrieked in terror. Persuaja's expression did not change.

The Zenda double looked just as shocked as the other girls. "Who are you?" she asked Zenda.

"Um, I can explain," Zenda said.

Two in One

Persuaja quickly took charge. First, she thrust the beartree branches into Alexandra's arms.

"Take these to Sabra immediately," she said. Alexandra nodded and ran off.

Then Persuaja turned to Sophia and the other girls.

"There is no need for alarm," she said. "Go back to your cabins. I will take care of this."

The girls quickly ran off. No one dared to question Persuaja—not even Sophia. Zenda cringed. She knew the story of the two Zendas would quickly spread to the other girls.

Persuaja turned to the two Zendas. "Follow me," she said.

When they reached Persuaja's cabin, the psychic sat both girls in chairs side by side. She pulled up a chair of her own across from them. She studied them both with a fascinated expression on her face.

"I have never seen a rendulla double before," she said. "The plant has been so closely protected for years now."

"It was an accident," the real Zenda said quickly.

"Was it?" Persuaja asked.

"The nocti got out," Zenda said. "I went into the woods to look for it. I lost track of time. And then I smelled the flower . . ."

Persuaja sighed. "Zenda, you know you should not have gone into the woods by yourself," she said. "I did not sense anything amiss until late last night, and even then I wasn't sure. I've been preoccupied lately."

The Zenda double stood up. "Would someone please explain what is going on here? Who is this girl? And why does she look like me—only dirtier?"

Persuaja looked amused. "Please sit down," she said to the Zenda double. "I will explain everything, in time."

"Fine," the double said, sitting down. She eyed the real Zenda uneasily.

"So you were telling me this was an

accident?" Persuaja asked.

"You're right. I shouldn't have gone into the woods on my own," Zenda admitted. "But I felt bad about the nocti. I didn't want anybody to be angry with me for letting it go."

"You should have told someone," Persuaja said.

"I know," Zenda said, throwing back her head in frustration. "I'm hopeless."

"No one expects you to be perfect," Persuaja said. "Not even after many years of working with your musings. All anyone expects is that you try your best."

There was a knock on the door. Persuaja stood up.

"That would be Alexandra with the potion ingredients," she said.

"How do you know that?" Zenda asked. "Is that a psychic thing?"

"Partly," Persuaja said. "And partly logic. You and your friends are clever, Zenda. I am sure you tried to solve this yourselves by making the antidote."

She opened the door, and Alexandra stood there with the two cloth sacks.

"I thought I should bring these," Alexandra said. "We tried to make a potion—"

"I know," Persuaja said, taking the sacks from her.

"What potion?" the double asked. "What are you talking about?"

"You were clever enough to make a potion to cure the effects of the rendulla flower," Persuaja said.

"I didn't make any potion," the double protested.

"Ah, but you did," Persuaja said. "You may be here in two bodies, but you are one person. Of course, you are more of a hope of a person than a real person."

The double frowned. "This doesn't make any sense. How can I be a hope of a person?"

"You are the person Zenda hopes to be," Persuaja said. "Or at least, the person she hoped to be at one time. That may have changed."

"Persuaja, am I really the same as her?" Zenda asked. She glanced at the double, not wanting to hurt her feelings. "I mean, the book said she is who I hope to be. But if I change my mind, I can always be some other way, can't I?"

"You can be whatever you want to be," Persuaja replied. "The rendulla double has some lovely qualities, I think. You may choose to nurture those. There may be other qualities, however, that you reject."

Persuaja took the sacks to a table and began to lay out the contents.

"We found almost everything," Alexandra said. "But we're missing—"

"Lifewort leaf," Persuaja said. She walked to a table topped with jars and picked up one with green leaves floating in water. "It doesn't grow around here. But I brought some. You never know what will happen when a rendulla flower is around."

Persuaja put the potion ingredients in a jar and filled it with water from a nearby pitcher. She dropped the lifewort leaf in last. Then she strained the potion into a large mug.

Alexandra's eyes glittered with curiosity as she looked at the two Zendas. "Can I watch?" she asked.

"It is better if you do not," Persuaja said. "The sight may be upsetting to those not used to it. But thank you for the ingredients."

"You're welcome," Alexandra said, her voice filled with disappointment. "Good luck, Zen."

"Thanks," Zenda replied.

Persuaja handed the mug to Zenda. "You must drink the whole thing," she said.

Zenda looked down into the goblet. The liquid was a pale brown, and it smelled vaguely like dirt.

The double looked nervous. "What exactly is going to happen?" she asked.

Zenda had a sudden guilty feeling. She didn't especially like her double too much, but she didn't want her to disappear. That seemed, well, kind of cruel.

Persuaja sensed her worry. She reached out and took each girl by the hand.

"You two are one and the same," she said. "When the potion has been taken, balance will be restored. It is the nature of things."

Persuaja's words calmed Zenda, and they seemed to have the same effect on the double. Zenda held the mug to her lips.

"Uh, see you soon," she told the double. Then she drank.

The thin, musky-tasting liquid was not easy to get down. Zenda closed her eyes and took gulp after gulp. She just wanted this all to be over.

When she had drained the last drop, Zenda felt a lightness in her head. She opened her eyes.

She seemed to be floating in space. There was darkness all around her. Her double stood in front of her. They smiled at each other. Everything felt right, somehow.

She and the double walked toward each other. Zenda closed her eyes instinctively. When she opened them, she was back in Persuaja's cabin, seated in the chair.

The double was gone.

"Is that it?" she asked.

"Almost," Persuaja said. "I trust you will not go into the woods after midnight again?"

"No!" Zenda said quickly.

"I must tell you something, Zenda," Persuaja continued. "I know that you tried to see me the morning after the rendulla created your double. I hope you understand. I know you needed me. But Astrid needs more of me right now."

"I understand," Zenda said.

Persuaja turned her head to the side, as though she had heard something. Then she got up and walked to the door. She opened it, and Astrid stood there, looking timid and nervous.

"Is Zenda all right?" she asked.

Persuaja opened the door. "See for yourself."

Astrid stepped inside. "I heard something bad happened to Zenda. I thought it might be—"

"What happened to Zenda was of her own doing," Persuaja said. "But if you have something to say to Zenda, now might be a good time."

Astrid faced Zenda but was unable to look at her.

"It was my fault," she said. "I made you fall off the stump. It wasn't on purpose," she continued. "My powers are kind of . . . crazy. It's like I think something, and it happens. Or if I'm mad, things fall. Or water boils, or a wind blows things away . . . It's like things happen in response to my emotions. I can't control it."

But something still bothered Zenda. "So you really didn't mean to hurt me?"

Astrid took a deep breath. "You saved Persuaja. You are so good at everything. And you were balancing so well in *sela* class, and I couldn't balance at all. I guess I was jealous. The next thing I knew, the stump moved, and you fell. I'm sorry."

"It's okay," Zenda said, and she meant it. "I used to make all kinds of weird things happen with my *kani*. I still do."

"Nicely done," Persuaja said to Astrid. "It takes courage to apologize. And to accept an apology," she said, turning back to Zenda. "Why don't you go back to your cabin. I'm sure your friends are worried about you."

Zenda got up, feeling suddenly light. It felt good not to be hiding her secret anymore.

Astrid stayed behind with Persuaja, and Zenda ran to her cabin. She saw Camille outside, pacing back and forth nervously.

"Did it work?" Camille asked, running

up to her.

"Yes," Zenda said. "There's only one me."

Camille grinned, and Zenda suddenly saw her friend light up with an aura. It was the color of peach skin, with shades of orange streaked through. At the same moment, a feeling of relief mixed with happiness washed over Zenda. She knew, instinctively, that it came from Camille.

"Wow!" Zenda said. "I can see your aura. It's a relieved, happy kind of thing. Right?"

"Right!" Camille cried. "Zenda, you did it."

Zenda felt a wave of confidence rise up in her. Was this how her double felt? Well, from now on it was going to be how Zenda felt, too!

"Come on," Zenda said. "I really need a shower!"

Sunrise

I can't believe the Astral Summer is about to end! It went by so fast.

After a few days, everybody stopped talking about me and my double. Things went back to normal, mostly. Astrid still works with Persuaja a lot, and she doesn't really talk to me. I think she still feels bad about what happened. That's too bad, because I honestly understand what she's going through.

I'm glad Persuaja didn't get too angry with me or send me home early. She's still my friend, even if she can't be with me all the time. And Persuaja thinks I'm strong. That's pretty amazing.

I have decided to try to keep both my kani and my aura sight. It felt good to use my kani to help Kyomi. I know I'm good at it. And I think I can be good at aura sight, too. I just need practice.

I know it won't be easy. When school starts, I will have to study twice as hard as everybody else! I might not be able to do it. But I'm going to try. Like Persuaja said, I can try to do my best.

Cosmically yours,
Zenda

———⚬⚬⚬———

Zenda stepped outside, grabbing a handful of moonglow flowers from the bucket by the door. All of the girls were gathering in the center of the village, each carrying the glowing flowers. She found her friends and stood next to them.

"Ready?" Sabra asked.

"Ready!" the girls shouted back.

All at once, the girls threw their moon-glow flowers into the air. The flowers floated back to the ground like giant fireflies shimmering in the dark.

The sky above began to lighten. A golden glow appeared over the horizon. The rays of the sun seemed to push away the darkness.

A smile grew on Zenda's face as the sun rose higher. Even after a long hibernation, the sun always came back. It was the start of a new day, a new season, and a new time for Zenda. She wasn't sure what to expect in the weeks to come.

But she was ready.